Dear Parent:

Congratulations! Your child is taking the first steps on an exciting journey. The destination? Independent reading!

STEP INTO READING® will help your child get there. The program offers five steps to reading success. Each step includes fun stories and colorful art. There are also Step into Reading Sticker Books, Step into Reading Math Readers, Step into Reading Phonics Readers, Step into Reading Write-In Readers, and Step into Reading Phonics Boxed Sets—a complete literacy program with something to interest every child.

Learning to Read, Step by Step!

Ready to Read   Preschool–Kindergarten
• big type and easy words • rhyme and rhythm • picture clues
For children who know the alphabet and are eager to begin reading.

Reading with Help   Preschool–Grade 1
• basic vocabulary • short sentences • simple stories
For children who recognize familiar words and sound out new words with help.

Reading on Your Own   Grades 1–3
• engaging characters • easy-to-follow plots • popular topics
For children who are ready to read on their own.

Reading Paragraphs   Grades 2–3
• challenging vocabulary • short paragraphs • exciting stories
For newly independent readers who read simple sentences with confidence.

Ready for Chapters   Grades 2–4
• chapters • longer paragraphs • full-color art
For children who want to take the plunge into chapter books but still like colorful pictures.

STEP INTO READING® is designed to give every child a successful reading experience. The grade levels are only guides. Children can progress through the steps at their own speed, developing confidence in their reading, no matter what their grade.

Remember, a lifetime love of reading starts with a single step!

Thomas the Tank Engine & Friends™

CREATED BY BRITT ALLCROFT

Based on The Railway Series by The Reverend W Awdry.
© 2012 Gullane (Thomas) LLC.
Thomas the Tank Engine & Friends and Thomas & Friends are trademarks of
Gullane (Thomas) Limited.
HIT and the HIT Entertainment logo are trademarks of HIT Entertainment Limited.
All rights reserved. Published in the United States by Random House Children's Books,
a division of Random House, Inc., 1745 Broadway, New York, NY 10019, and in Canada by
Random House of Canada Limited, Toronto.

Step into Reading, Random House, and the Random House colophon are registered
trademarks of Random House, Inc.

Visit us on the Web!
StepIntoReading.com
randomhouse.com/kids
www.thomasandfriends.com

Educators and librarians, for a variety of teaching tools, visit us at
randomhouse.com/teachers

ISBN: 978-0-307-92996-9 (trade) — ISBN: 978-0-375-97003-0 (lib. bdg.)

Printed in the United States of America 10 9 8 7 6 5 4 3 2 1

STEP INTO READING®

STEP 2

Easter Engines

Based on The Railway Series
by The Reverend W Awdry

Illustrated by Richard Courtney

Random House  New York

It is Easter morning.
James, Percy, and Thomas
are being washed
for the Easter parade.

"We are bright and shiny, like Easter eggs!" says James.

Thomas is happy.
He will lead
the parade.

Suddenly,

Sir Topham Hatt arrives.

He has an important job

for Thomas.

Thomas must go
to McColl's Farm.
He must get
an Easter egg.

Thomas will do
the job.
Then he will race
back to the parade.

Thomas zooms
down the track.

He sees

McColl's Farm.

Thomas stops
at the farm.
He is surprised!

The egg is very shiny.
It is also very big!

"It is the biggest egg
in the world!"
says Thomas.

Terence tells Thomas
to be careful.
He tells Thomas
not to break the egg.

Chug. Chug.

Thomas rolls slowly up the track.

He is very careful.

He does not want

to break the egg.

The egg shakes
and wobbles.
It does not fall.

Quack! Quack!

Thomas stops.

He lets the ducks

cross the track.

Thomas reaches
the parade.
It is almost over!

Thomas is not
the first engine
in the parade.
He is the last engine.

But the children cheer
for Thomas!

The children cheer
for the giant egg!

The parade is over.
"How did the egg
get so big?"
asks Thomas.

Sir Topham Hatt
chuckles.
The egg is not real.
It is made of paper!

Rip! Rip!
Sir Topham Hatt
opens the egg.
It is full
of Easter baskets!

One child gives Thomas
a basket!
Thomas is very happy.

The children love
their baskets.
They thank Thomas.

"We are like big,
shiny eggs,"
James says to Thomas.

"But you are like
a big Easter bunny!"
says Percy.

"Happy Easter!"
says Thomas.